P9-BUI-343

TRAILBLAZERS
Telling Tall Tales
in Tennessee

by Jesse Leon McCann
Illustrated by Duendes del Sur

SCHOLASTIC INC.

New York Toronto London Auckland Sydney
Mexico City New Delhi Hong Kong Buenos Aires

This book is a work of hysterical fiction. Any similarities to actual historical persons, places, or events are likely to be wacky. In other words: don't use this book for a history report!

Published by Scholastic Inc.,
90 Old Sherman Turnpike,
Danbury, Connecticut 06816.

0-439-56591-X

Printed in the U.S.A.
First printing, February 2004

CONTENTS

• • • • • • • • • • • • •

This Is the Story, F-F-Folks!

Porky Pig here. I have a story to tell you that's pretty amazing. It all started when the ACME Space Replacer arrived here at the Warner Bros. Movie Studios. (Those of us who work here call it the WB Studio for short.) Now, we've used products made by the ACME Company for years in our shows. But the ACME Space Replacer is d-d-different from any other ACME product. The Space Replacer can take us wherever we want, and we can go back or forward in time, too.

Oh, and in case you don't know, by *us* and *we,* I mean me and the other characters I work with here at the WB Studio. For instance, in this story, you'll meet Daffy Duck, a very nice fellow and a major talent—if you don't mind someone who always thinks of himself first and throws a tantrum when things don't go his way.

Oh, y-y-yes, there's something else that's very important. To return to our own place and time, we need a special watchlike gadget called the Re-replacer. Not only does the Re-replacer tell us lots of information about the place we're visiting, but it also tells us where we have to be and when we have to be there so that the Re-replacer can beam us home.

One time, Daffy and I visited outer space using the Space Replacer. Another time, we stumbled upon a top-secret experiment right here on Earth—in the 1940s. We've even gone back to the time of King Arthur and the Knights of the Round Table. It's all been very exciting. In this adventure, Daffy and I used the Space Replacer to visit the American frontier. I wanted to meet folk legends, but Daffy was only interested in finding Davy Crockett's treasure. As it turned out, we both got our way. Read on to find out how.

Porky Pig

Two Saps and a Map

Porky Pig walked through the Warner Bros. lot, waving good-naturedly to friends and coworkers as he made his way to the studio post office. He passed the famous Warner water tower and turned left at The Big Boss's office building. Then he turned right at the cafeteria, where actors and crew were eating lunch. Finally, Porky went happily up to the post office doors—and was run over from behind by Daffy Duck.

POW!

"Out of my way, Meathead! Important duck on important business coming through!" Daffy knocked Porky head-over-curly tail. Daffy wasn't as popular as Porky around the studio— or anywhere else for that matter. He was vain, greedy, conniving, and hotheaded.

Porky skidded to a stop. Ignoring him, Daffy quickly pulled out his key ring and fumbled for the key to his post office box. "Let's see, sports car, sauna, pastry pantry, action figure display case . . . " he said, as he thumbed through his many keys.

"Gee, Daffy," said Porky, as he pulled out the key to his own post office box and opened it. "I know it's fun to get fan mail, but you don't have to mow a guy down!" Inside Porky's box, there was a mountain of fan letters. After all, his fans loved him. Daffy gave a sour look and opened his own box. There was only one letter inside. Porky couldn't help but smile.

"Laugh it up, Mr. Popular," Daffy said snidely. "I'll have you know, this is better than any fan letter you've ever gotten. It's something I bought in an Internet auction!"

Daffy ripped open the letter and pulled out the contents. "This is it," Daffy declared, his eyes shining. "I'll be rich, affluent, well-to-do—exceedingly comfortable!"

"What's the big deal, Daffy?" Porky asked, carrying his big bundle of fan letters out the door. "It just looks like an old piece of tree bark with some writing and pictures on it."

"Are you kidding?" Daffy asked, following Porky outside. "This just happens to be an old trailblazer's treasure map from 1806, which clearly marks the spot where a fantastic gold treasure is buried!"

"Oh, Daffy, I can't believe you fell for that," said Porky. "A lot of what they sell in those auctions is just not real."

"This is real!" Daffy pulled out a paper that came with the map. "It even came with a letter of proof. See? It was signed by Mr. D. Crockett in 1806."

"*Davy Crockett?* The great frontiersman?" Porky cried. "Let me see!" Porky was a big fan of historical legends and heroes from American folklore. He glanced at the tree bark, hoping to get a look at the famous man's signature. But Daffy quickly pulled the map away.

"Oh no! A minute ago, you laughed at my map!" Daffy sneered, then his face took on a thoughtful look. "Although, I might let you *hold* it, if you give me a quick lift somewhere. My car is in the shop."

"I'd be glad to," Porky exclaimed excitedly.

"On second thought . . . no, I could not possibly intrude," Daffy said, starting to walk away.

"I'm happy to help," replied Porky eagerly. Now he was following Daffy across the lot.

"No, I'm sure a big star like you is *much* too busy," Daffy said, smiling to himself. He was playing Porky like a finely tuned violin.

"Not at all," Porky said. He was beginning to fear he'd never get a look at Davy Crockett's map.

"You're just being kind," said Daffy.

"It's not a problem," said Porky. "By the way, where do you need to go?"

"Tennessee," Daffy said, smiling sweetly. "It's only a *few* thousand miles."

Minutes later Daffy was loading Porky's jalopy with stuff. While Porky had just one small overnight bag, Daffy was bringing along five suitcases, two garment bags, a duffel bag, a makeup case, a trunk of 8-inch by 10-inch photographs (in case somebody asked for an autograph), and something that was wrapped in a blanket. Daffy tied the large, mysterious item onto the roof of Porky's car.

"I always like to travel light," Daffy said, hopping into the passenger seat next to Porky. "So, let's make like a banana and split!"

Porky was a slow, careful driver. Before they had even gotten out of Hollywood, Daffy was getting restless. "Move over, I'm driving!" he shouted. Before Porky could protest, Daffy pushed him over and took the steering wheel. Daffy zoomed out of the city, over the mountains, and into the desert.

Porky wanted to stop in Las Vegas. "No deal," said Daffy.

Porky wanted to see the Grand Canyon. Daffy brushed him off.

Porky wanted to take a look at the Painted Desert. *"No!"* Daffy yelled.

They rushed! They sped! They got to Tennessee as fast as physically possible. Soon they were entering the town of Tiptonville, Tennessee, where the X on the map indicated Davy Crockett had stashed his treasure of gold.

Daffy was giddy with excitement. "I'm going to be a tycoon, a player—I'll be eminently wealthy!" he exclaimed.

But Daffy's smile left his beak when they drew close to where the map said the treasure would be. The spot was covered by a five-story building. If the treasure was under there, it was covered by tons of concrete and steel.

Porky thought Daffy handled the disappointment surprisingly well—he only cried and pounded the ground, screaming, *"Why, why, why?"* for a few minutes. Then the plucky duck calmly got to his feet and fetched the mysterious item from Porky's car roof. He quickly unwrapped it.

It was the Space Replacer.

The Space Replacer was a machine that could send anyone to any place at any time. Bugs and Daffy had taken the Space Replacer to visit Caribbean pirates. Porky and Daffy had used it to travel to another planet. Now Daffy was planning to go back in time to get Davy Crockett's treasure.

"For crying out loud, Daffy," Porky said, sighing. "If you had the Space Replacer, why didn't you use it to get to Tennessee in the first place?"

"Well, if you must know, I vowed only to use it again if I absolutely had to," said Daffy. He typed in where he wanted to go and what year he wanted it to be. "The last time I got Space Replaced, I barely got back with my feathers intact!"

Next Daffy strapped the Re-replacer unit onto his wrist. The Re-replacer was very important. They would need it not only to get back home but also to obtain tons of valuable information. *"Next stop, 1806!"* Daffy declared, grabbing Porky, who was trying to sneak away.

As soon as Daffy pushed the big red button

on the Space Replacer, a bright light appeared all around them. Their modern-day surroundings melted away. Things shifted, then came back into focus.

The air seemed fresher, the environment more open. They heard the sound of rapidly rushing water. The ground seemed to move and tilt. Then they realized they were on a rickety old raft, careening swiftly down a river!

CHAPTER 2
Mississippi Sissy

A man was trying to steer the raft with a long, thin pole. Waves crashed dangerously against the raft. The man looked nervous and was crying out for help!

Daffy was getting seasick. "Great! We're in danger and *he's* driving?" Daffy moaned. "Who is this guy, anyway?"

"Use the Re-replacer," suggested Porky.

Daffy pointed the Re-replacer at the man, then he pressed the white button. These words appeared on its screen:

The Legend of Mike Fink

Mike Fink was the greatest river-raft pilot there ever was. He was known for his bold speech, incredible strength, limitless bravery, and amazing aim with a pistol.

"Mike Fink?" Porky said. "He doesn't look like the Mike Fink *I've* read about. He's so sm-sm-small. And not very brave."

"Boy, you're telling me!" Daffy muttered, clinging to the raft. It shook and skimmed over the choppy water. "I may be a duck, but that guy is a chicken!"

As the river swept around a bend, Mike barely missed steering them into a pile of boulders. **"Help!"** he cried again. **"I want my mommy!"**

"That does it!" Daffy announced, fighting to keep his balance as he approached Mike. "I'm taking over this river cruise!"

"Now, Daffy, Mike can handle this," Porky hollered over the crashing water. "After all, the legend says . . . "

Mike seemed to notice them for the first time. "*Aaaah!* River bandits come to steal my raft!" shouted Mike. **"Help! Help!"** He let go of the pole and ran around in circles.

"Yeah, he's a real hero," Daffy scoffed. Daffy took the pole, but the current was very strong. He flew back and forth as the pole swung wildly. *"Help!"* he cried.

Porky grabbed hold of the pole, too. He was able to stop Daffy's erratic swinging, but the raft was still out of control. Porky reached out and grabbed Mike.

"Come on, Mike!" encouraged Porky. "You're a legend, I know you can save us."

"Eeeeek! Don't hurt me!" Mike shrieked.

With Daffy frantically pulling in one direction and Porky trying to get Mike to steer the other way, they managed to avoid breaking the raft up. The churning water spun them around backward. Daffy's wild steering almost tipped them over. "What a b-b-bad day!" Porky said with a sigh.

Suddenly they hit a part of the river where the water turned white with rushing foam. It was choppy, with even more boulders than before, and it dropped suddenly in several places. As they rounded a bend, Porky and Daffy saw that a huge tree had fallen across the river. The water flowed easily under it but, if they didn't duck immediately, they'd be knocked into the dangerous water for sure. Porky and Daffy leaped onto the tree just as the raft slid under it.

But Mike hadn't seen the tree until it was about to hit him. At that moment he fainted. Lying passed out on the raft, he glided easily under the fallen tree. The pole, though, was smashed away.

The noise from the crash woke Mike. He stood up, looked back at the tree, and scratched his head in confusion. At that spot, the Mississippi River suddenly became much calmer. The raft began to drift smoothly, even without a pole to steer with.

As Daffy and Porky watched cowardly Mike Fink float away, they heard an astonished voice behind them say, "Don't tell me you just rafted here down the mighty Mississippi!" They turned to see a grizzled old man, leaning on a sign that read **WELCOME TO MEMPHIS**. The man looked at them with wondering eyes.

"Well, yes, we did," replied Porky, as he and Daffy walked onto the nearby riverbank.

"And that man yonder was the pilot?" the old-timer asked, pointing in the distance to Mike Fink on his raft. "He must be the greatest river rafter who ever lived."

"Oh, yeah. Mike Fink is a *real* legend!" scoffed Daffy.

"A legend, eh?" said the old man, who didn't understand that Daffy was being sarcastic. He looked at Mike—who was floating away downriver—with deep respect. That part of the Mississippi was the most dangerous. No one could raft through it. He figured this Mike Fink was amazing.

"Just wait 'til I tell the fellers about the great

Mike Fink!" the old man called out as he turned and hobbled quickly toward the small town. "He'll become a legend around here."

"No, I didn't mean he was really a legend . . . ," Daffy yelled after him, but the man had already disappeared.

"I think what you said to that old man is what started the legend of Mike Fink in the first place," Porky said. "He thinks Mike Fink did all the steering and is a great raft pilot because of us."

"Typical," Daffy muttered, rolling his eyes. "I do all the work and get none of the glory. Well, now what? Let's see what the Re-replacer has to say." He pushed the black button and words appeared on the screen:

WHERE: western Tennessee
WHEN: 1806
WHO: 2 travelers
TIME REMAINING: 3 days,
2 hours, 2 minutes, 45 seconds
RETURN CHECKPOINT: Davy Crockett's cabin, Tiptonville, Tennessee

"At last, a stroke of good luck!" exclaimed Daffy. "The Space Replacer return checkpoint is right where the gold treasure is!"

"We've got 3 days and a lot of traveling to do," Porky said. "Tiptonville is pretty far away, and we'll need provisions and directions. We'd better go into town."

As Porky and Daffy entered the town, they met the old man again and asked him how to get to Tiptonville. "This here trail will take you in the direction you need to go. Step lightly and make sure you keep an eye out for bears!" the old man warned.

As they walked along the trail, Porky looked around nervously. **"Bears?"** he cried. "I don't like the idea of meeting bears in the forest!"

"Aw, that old geezer was just trying to scare you, Porky," Daffy said with a smirk. "The likelihood of us running into a bear this close to town is zero—especially on a trail in the middle of the day. Besides, bears aren't so tough!"

Just then two cute baby bears wandered out of the woods and onto the path in front of them.

"*Aaaah! Bears!*" screamed Daffy. He jumped around like a yo-yo on a rubber band and ran screaming into the woods.

Porky chuckled. "Who could be frightened of two such cuddly little guys? Although it does seem odd that they would wander around all by themselves," he added, as the bear cubs ambled up to him and he patted their heads. "That is, if they *are* by themselves."

At that moment a ferocious growl came from the woods nearby. Seconds later a gigantic mother bear thundered through the trees and stood on the path in front of Porky.

Porky ran for his life, climbing hills and crawling under fallen logs. The mama bear stayed right on his tail, angrily swiping at him with her sharp claws. Her cubs followed behind her.

Porky leaped behind a bush—and crashed into Daffy, who was hiding there. "Thanks a lot!" snarled Daffy. "You gave away my hiding place!"

The mama bear came crashing through the underbrush, just missing them with her claws. Porky and Daffy jumped up and ran as fast as their feet could carry them, but the bear drew closer and closer. They quickly scurried up a tree, leaving the bear and her cubs down below.

"*Whew!*" Daffy said. "That was a close one."

"Daffy," said Porky. "Can't bears climb trees?" Together, they looked down just as the mama bear started climbing up the tree. They moved toward the next branch, which was about 20 feet in the air. As they looked up at the branch they were heading for, they saw a young man sitting there, giving them a friendly smile. Porky and Daffy reached the branch, then sat down next to the young man to catch their breath.

"Howdy! Nice day, ain't it?" the young man said slowly. He held a rifle and was dressed in buckskin with a coonskin cap. "Pleased to meet you. My name is Davy Crockett."

CHAPTER 4

Porky's Hero

"Davy Crockett?" Porky repeated, grinning. "Why, you're one of my heroes!"

"Hey," Daffy interrupted sourly. "I hate to break up your love fest, but have you forgotten we have a killer bear right below us?"

"Aw, bears don't concern me none," drawled Davy. "I've gotten out of many a scrape with bears." Then he slowly started to fill his rifle with gunpowder.

Daffy shouted, "Then do something! We're sitting ducks up here—well, I am, anyway."

"Reckon I *am* doing something," Davy said, continuing to pour the powder.

Sweat running down his face, Daffy glanced below. The bear was getting closer by the second. "How about doing something *faster?*" he urged.

Porky was still fascinated by the fact that Davy Crockett was right there next to him. "You know, I've read dozens of books about you, Davy," he said.

"Look, write him a fan letter later!" Daffy complained. Then getting down on his knees, he began to beg. "Please, Davy, shoot that bear! Please, please, please!"

"Can't, I reckon," Davy said. He finished pouring and put away his sack of gunpowder.

"Why not?" cried Daffy.

"Ain't got any bullets," Davy said calmly. "Can't shoot a rifle without bullets."

The bear was only inches below them now. "Then why did you spend all that time filling the barrel with gunpowder?" Daffy asked. The bear reared back and raised one paw.

"I filled my rifle with powder so I can do this," Davy said, holding up the rifle and pulling the trigger. The flint lit the powder with a flash.

POW!

Frightened by the sudden sound, the mama bear scurried back down the tree, took her youngsters, and fled. Daffy and Porky were saved!

Soon after, they had climbed down the tree and were walking along the path. "That was very br-br-bril—smart, Davy!" Porky said, beaming. "You really are clever!"

"He really is a moron, is what he is," Daffy grumbled. "Not only did he almost get me killed, but he scared the heck out of me with that popgun."

"Oh, yeah? I think this might change your mind," Porky argued as he grabbed Daffy's wrist and quickly pushed a button on the Re-replacer:

The Life of Davy Crockett
Famous frontiersman. Became a U.S. congressman in 1827. Hero of the Alamo during the war for Texas's independence.
Now, who's a moron?

Daffy pointed a thumb at the gawky young Davy. "It's kind of hard to believe he'll do all those things. But if he's such a great frontier guy, maybe he can lead us to Tiptonville," Daffy hinted.

"Sure, I reckon I can," Davy said. "In fact, I have a cabin in the woods there. I'd show it to you, but I can't remember where it is."

"*This* is our frontier guide?" snorted Daffy. "He can't even find his own house!"

"Oh, I got lots of cabins in the woods," Davy explained. "In fact, I have to draw maps to remind me where they're at. It's just that I lost the map to my Tiptonville place."

Suddenly Daffy realized that the map to Davy's cabin was the treasure map he was carrying. He pulled out the map and studied it eagerly. If Davy could get them to Tiptonville, Daffy could follow the map to the treasure!

"Well, I'll be!" Davy exclaimed when he saw Daffy's map. "That there looks just like the map I lost. Now, doesn't that beat all?"

"You know how it is, once you've seen one map, you've seen them all," said Daffy. He put on a phony smile and quickly put the map away.

They hiked through the woods until the sun began to set. "I suggest we make camp for the night by that creek over there," Daffy said, pointing.

"That's not a good idea, Daffy," Porky explained. "Bears and wolves like to hunt for smaller animals by a creek. It would be better to find higher ground up on that hill."

"Up there?" Daffy cried. "I'm exhausted and not doing any more climbing today!" As they argued, they suddenly realized that Davy had disappeared.

"Davy! Where are you?" Porky called. "Oh, this could be b-b-bad!"

"That's okay, who needs him?"

Daffy said. He noticed a soft glow of light a few hundred feet away. "Look, there's a campfire! We can camp with whoever that is!"

Daffy grabbed Porky by the arm and pulled him through the woods toward the campfire. "Boy, I can't wait to get a good night's sleep!" said Daffy, as they came into the firelight. "Hello, strangers! I hope you don't mind if we share your . . ."

Suddenly Daffy froze with fear. Porky gulped. Around the campfire sat several Native American braves. They looked up at the intruders with stern eyes.

CHAPTER 5

Folklore and Apple Cores

"*Hello, there!*" said one brave. "Come rest and sit by the fire."

Porky blinked. "You speak English?" he asked.

"Sure," answered the brave. "This is America, isn't it?" The braves told Daffy and Porky that they were members of the Chickasaw nation, a very large tribe.

Daffy consulted the Re-replacer:

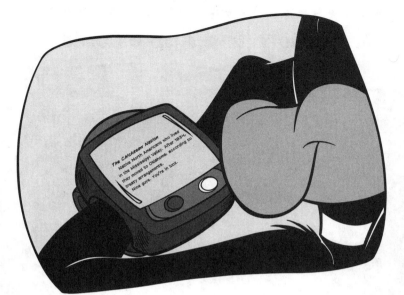

The Chickasaw Nation

Native North Americans who lived in the Mississippi Valley. After 1834, they moved to Oklahoma, according to treaty arrangements.

Nice guys. You're in luck.

The Chickasaw shared their food and blankets with Daffy and Porky and told them stories around the campfire. Daffy was so happy that the braves were peaceful that he volunteered to do a rain dance for them. The Chickasaw watched politely, but Porky could tell they thought Daffy was crazy.

The next morning, the Chickasaw took them to the border of their hunting grounds. Now Porky and Daffy were a lot closer to their goals: the gold treasure and the Space Replacer return checkpoint.

Daffy checked the Re-replacer—they still had two days to get to Tiptonville. They continued on their way until they came to a place where they had to cross a river. "The river current looks rather p-p-pow—very strong," Porky said anxiously.

"Luckily, I have brains as well as good looks," Daffy said. "We won't go in the water. We'll cross on those rocks over there." Daffy started hopping across some wet stones that peeked out of the river. "See, nothing to it," he bragged. But halfway across, he wobbled and then fell into the water with a loud splash!

Daffy's feathers were so wet and ruffled that Porky couldn't help but laugh. *"Ha, ha, ha! Very funny!"* Daffy said. "I'd like to see you do better." Porky skipped across the stepping stones to the other side of the river without getting a drop of water on him. "You're *despicable*," grumbled Daffy, as he paddled to shore.

Porky waded into the river and helped Daffy stagger the rest of the way to shore. Just then Porky noticed that the Re-replacer was wet. "Oh, d-d-dear," he cried. "I hope it still works." He unstrapped it from Daffy's wrist and put it on. "I'd better hold it for a while," Porky suggested. "I think it will be safer with me."

By the time the sun was high in the sky that afternoon, their stomachs were grumbling loudly. Luckily, they came upon a burlap sack sitting beside the path they were following. It was full of ripe, delicious apples!

Daffy and Porky dug right in, hungrily eating apple after apple until there were just a few left. They were biting into two more apples when they noticed a stranger standing over them, frowning angrily. Gulping down the last pieces of apple, they froze.

The man had a wild beard and was dressed in only his long johns. He wore a cooking pot on his head and was walking around with no shoes on his feet. "Do you know how long it took me to pick all them apples?" the man yelled. "Now you've gone and eaten almost every one!"

Daffy and Porky started picking up all the apple cores and putting them in the sack. But the stranger was furious! He stomped and sputtered and kicked and stamped.

Suddenly Porky's eyes went wide. He knew who this crazy man was! **"Hey!"** he cried, "I recognize you! You're Johnny—"

"Bag-of-Apples!" the man finished.

"What?" Porky asked, confused.

"That's right, I'm Johnny Bag-of-Apples!" said the man. "My life's work is to go all over this great country and give people apples out of my bag. But it's really hard to find apples *and then have you go and eat 'em!*" With that, Johnny started stomping and sputtering again.

Daffy scowled at Porky and whined, "Don't tell me this guy is another of your legends."

"Yep, he's another folk legend," Porky said.

"To me, he looks more like a nut in his underwear," said Daffy. He tapped Johnny on the shoulder. "Hey, fuzzy! I hate to break it to you, but we did you a favor. Now all you have to do is take this sack of apple cores and plant the seeds all over the country. Soon, there'll be so many apple trees, you'll have plenty of fruit."

Johnny suddenly stopped his grumbling and thought about what Daffy had said.

"Sheesh," Daffy said, rolling his eyes. "I mean, you don't have to be a *rocket scientist* to figure that one out."

"And then you can call yourself Johnny Appleseed," Porky said with a smile.

"What a fantastic idea!" cheered Johnny. "Except for the Johnny Appleseed part. That's a dumb name. 'Sides, I'm mighty partial to Johnny Bag-of-Apples." Then Johnny grabbed his bag of apple seeds and ran away shouting, "Wait 'til I tell the fellers in town about this!"

"Boy, you sure know how to pick 'em, Porky," Daffy said, as they continued up the trail. "That guy was a few apples short of a bushel!"

By the time they had reached the next settlement hours later, the place was buzzing with news about Johnny. Everywhere they went, they heard people talking.

"Did you hear about Johnny Bag-of-Apples?"

"He's going to plant apple seeds all across the nation! He'll be famous!"

"I hear somebody once called him Johnny Appleseed."

"Now, that's a right good name!"

Daffy couldn't believe he'd taken part in the creation of *another* folklore legend.

Tired and hungry, Daffy and Porky went into a nearby eatery to get some dinner. To their great surprise, Davy Crockett was sitting there, smiling at them. "There you are," said Davy.

He seemed to be expecting them. "What took you so long?"

"Why did you leave?" Porky asked as they sat down.

"I just reckoned you fellers were doin' some trading with the Chickasaw," Davy explained. "And since I didn't need to trade, I just kept walkin'."

"I just kept walkin'," mimicked Daffy. He was furious with Davy for leaving. Daffy moaned about it until it was time for bed.

CHAPTER 6
Buffalo Crossing

The next morning, Daffy was still angry. "We weren't in danger but you didn't know that! Some hero of the wild frontier you are! I've seen better heroes on boxes of cereal! No, sir, I'd never vote for you for Hero of the Month." Even as the threesome began following a trail through the woods, Daffy kept on complaining.

"Your partner sure does gripe a lot," Davy quietly remarked to Porky.

"You have no idea," said Porky, as he checked the Re-replacer. He saw that they had only 1 day, 1 hour, and 52 minutes left.

"That there's a right pretty bracelet, Porky," Davy said. He looked closely at the Re-replacer. "And *lookee* at all them numbers and words and whatnot!"

They came out of the woods and entered a beautiful plain of tall grass. It was so quiet that Porky could clearly hear birds chirping. "I been thinking real hard about that map you got, Daffy," Davy said suddenly. "I swear on my pappy's porch chair it looks *'xactly* like the one I lost a week or so ago."

"Do tell? Well, don't think *too* hard, Einstein," Daffy grumbled. "You might strain your pea brain."

"You see, it was a map to my cabin in Tiptonville, where I stashed my golden treasure," continued Davy. "I wonder if I might have a look-see at that map again."

"Nothing doing, Bub!" Daffy shouted, crossing his arms stubbornly. "I paid good money for that map and it's mine!"

"Don't feel too bad, Davy," Porky said. "Here, this will cheer you up. You can wear the Re-replacer for a while, since you like it so much."

"Gee! Thanks," Davy said while Porky strapped the Re-replacer onto his wrist.

"Are you crazy?" yelled Daffy. "If he breaks that, we'll be stuck here forever!"

"Davy won't hurt it!" Porky argued.

"He'd better not!"

"He won't!"

"Quiet," Davy shushed them. But they continued to argue, so he said it again, a bit more firmly, **"Quiet, fellers!"**

Daffy was offended. "What? How dare you!" he shouted. "Back home, I happen to be a big movie star—" Daffy stopped. Now he heard it, too. A low rumble in the distance was getting louder. They stood frozen. The sound got louder and louder. "What's all the hubbub . . . Bub?" Daffy croaked softly.

The sound became deafening. Davy suddenly screamed, **"Stampede!"**

They ran through the grass

as fast as they could. When they'd reached a place where the grass wasn't so tall, Porky glanced behind them. Hundreds of buffalo were stampeding toward them!

"You done scared them with all your loud arguing!" cried Davy.

"*We* scared *them?*" squawked Daffy.

"I suggest we all r-r-run!" cried Porky.

Porky, Daffy, and Davy scrambled out of the buffalo's path. When the stampede had passed, Porky and Daffy were dusty but unhurt. They looked around for Davy. Strangely, he was nowhere in sight. "I sure hope he didn't get trampled by the buffalo," Porky said.

"He's just disappeared," Daffy noted. Suddenly Daffy's eyes went wide.

"W-w-what's the matter?" asked Porky.

"Davy's gone," Daffy cried, "and he was wearing the Re-replacer!"

CHAPTER 7
Going for the Gold

That night, Daffy and Porky slept a few hours on the edge of the plain they had crossed. Early the next morning, they stumbled up the dusty trail until they reached the tiny town of Tiptonville. The town was little more than a trading post and a few farmhouses.

Tired and hungry, they entered the trading post. Despite the early hour, the place was full of angry-looking frontiersmen. Daffy and Porky sat down to rest. When they heard what the men were talking about, they became very, very nervous.

"That buffalo stampede ruined a full day of huntin', maybe more!" growled a hunter.

"That's nothin'!" cried a trapper crossly. "The beavers at the creek swam an' hid as soon as the rumblin' started!"

"You should see my crops!" a grouchy farmer shouted. "Ruined by them buffalo!"

"Maybe some strangers crossed the plain yesterday and didn't have enough fool sense to keep quiet!" exclaimed a particularly large man.

Porky and Daffy gulped. Suddenly the men in the trading post turned to stare at them.

"Why, you two is strangers!" said an old

man sourly. "Maybe it's you who done it!"

The men got up and walked toward them threateningly. "Now . . . now, hold on, everybody," Porky said.

"You got it all wrong," Daffy said. "We saw the man who caused the stampede. He was a real mean dude with the strength of ten men!"

"Yeah?" the men said.

"Oh, yeah!" said Daffy. "He rode a mountain lion, used a rattler for a bullwhip, and lassoed a twister, he did!"

The men were wide-eyed. Daffy had their full attention. "Then he rode that twister like it was a rodeo bull! He let loose a howl that shook the ground! That's when the buffalo decided to run for it!"

At that moment a mild-mannered accountant, who had traveled from New York to set up a practice in the West, walked in through the doors of the trading post. He was a tall, frail, thin gentleman who looked as though he'd blow away in a heavy wind.

Daffy pointed at the man and screamed, "That's the guy, right there!"

The local men surrounded the man. Fearing that the men would hurt the stranger, Porky was about to admit that he and Daffy were the real culprits. But instead of being angry with the skinny man, the locals were fascinated by him and by the story Daffy had told.

"What's your name, stranger?" the trapper asked.

"It's Bill," said the man. "But I think I might change my name to *Pecos* Bill since I'm a Westerner now!"

"Three cheers for Pecos Bill, the rootin', tootin' high plains honcho!" the locals shouted. **"Hooray!"** They lifted the surprised Pecos Bill onto their shoulders and carried him away.

Dumbfounded, Daffy looked at Porky and suddenly realized what he had done. "Don't tell

me," he said. "I just turned *another* wimp into an American folk legend, didn't I?"

"Yep," said Porky, smiling.

Furious, Daffy stormed out of the trading post. He couldn't even make *himself* into a legend! It wasn't fair that all these people were benefiting from what he had said!

Suddenly Porky remembered their missing Re-replacer. They couldn't return to the WB Studio without it.

"Aw, the heck with it!" Daffy muttered, pulling out the map. "Let's go find the treasure. If we can't go back, at least I'm going to be rich!" When it came to gold, Daffy wasn't going to let anything stop him. With a determined stride, Daffy set off following the map's directions, with Porky running behind.

They climbed hills and struggled through underbrush. By the time they spotted Davy's cabin, they were exhausted. But Daffy got a sudden burst of energy when he remembered the riches inside. **_"There it is! The gold is inside! And it's mine, all mine!"_** Daffy cried frantically. **_"I'm rich! Rich, I say! Incredibly opulent! Exceedingly affluent!"_**

Dragging Porky along, Daffy ran to the cabin, just as fast as his greedy legs could take him. He tore open the door, raced inside—and found Davy Crockett sitting there smiling. "Howdy, fellers," said Davy. "I been waitin' for you all day."

"What the hey?" Daffy said. "I thought you didn't know where this place was?"

Davy pulled out the Re-replacer. "Oh, this here funny bracelet helped me find my way. It's got a powerful good compass." He handed the Re-replacer back to Porky.

Porky quickly pushed the black button:

WHERE: western Tennessee
WHEN: 1806
WHO: 2 travelers
TIME REMAINING: 2 minutes,
10 seconds
RETURN CHECKPOINT: Davy
Crockett's cabin, Tiptonville,
Tennessee

"Never mind that!" screeched Daffy.
"Where's all the gold?"

"Reckon it's right here." Davy gestured all
around the inside of the cabin.

Porky and Daffy noticed the entire cabin was filled with drying stalks of golden corn, and sacks of golden cornmeal were stacked to the ceiling.

"I want to thank you fellers for helpin' me find it," Davy politely said, grinning. "Ain't nothin' like a storehouse of golden corn to last you through a cold winter."

Daffy was stunned, then he began to shake and sputter, **"NO . . . no . . . NO!"** He threw himself into a tantrum.

Porky was worried. If Daffy didn't calm down, he might not be in the Space Replacer's laser beam when it came for them. "Davy, could you help me do something?" Porky asked.

"Sure, Pardner," agreed Davy, "anything you say."

Porky took a rope off the wall of the cabin. They surrounded Daffy and did their work. They finished just as the laser beam came to return them to the future. Daffy let out a muffled sob. Porky waved good-bye to Davy.

ZAP!

Once back in the present, Porky helped Daffy into the backseat of his car. Soon they were back on the road, heading for Hollywood at a nice, slow pace. Porky wouldn't have to worry about Daffy's crazy driving on this trip.

"Maybe we'll even stop off and see a few sights on the way back. After all, we're in no hurry," thought Porky. "Hmm . . . isn't it peaceful?"

Porky turned to check on Daffy. The duck was still struggling in the backseat. But Daffy was secure.

"Good old Davy Crockett!" Porky thought and smiled. "He sure knew how to tie a knot!"